P9-CJY-196

Celebrating  Years

The Very Hungry Caterpillar

50 Years of The Very Hungry Caterpillar

An Appreciation of Eric Carle
by Dolly Parton

Over the years, I have often been asked if I just had a feeling that a song I was writing would be a hit or, for heaven's sake, even a classic. When I wrote "Coat of Many Colors," I thought it was a special song but only because it was special to me. I had no idea if it would mean much to anyone else.

The original 1969 cover, before Eric Carle re-created the art using more modern, colorfast materials

When he wrote *The Very Hungry Caterpillar*, I bet Eric didn't know he was making a classic, but I feel confident he knew that he was creating a very special book because, again, the book was very special to him. He gave it to the world, and the children around the world made it a classic.

Eric has given millions of children a memory so many of us share. Our little cabin in the mountains became a magical place when my mother read stories to me. The light was dim, the fire was bright and the quilt wrapped around me felt like my own warm, loving cocoon. It was a deeply emotional experience for me that will last forever. As writers and artists, we all dream our work will create these beautiful moments over and over again.

I certainly know this is what we are trying to do with our Imagination Library. We work hard every day to inspire children to love reading and learning. I know millions of children have enjoyed *The Very Hungry Caterpillar*, but at the same time, millions of children have not had the opportunity to hold the book in their hands. Every child should hear, see and touch books like *The Very Hungry Caterpillar*. This is the moment when the dreams of children are born.

It is hard to imagine what our world will be like when *The Very Hungry Caterpillar* turns 100 years old. Some think books as we know them will simply not exist. Not me! I know that as long as there are children, a little hand will hold a well-worn copy of *The Very Hungry Caterpillar* and a precious little face will look up and say, "Please read it to me again!"

Love,
Dolly

Chairperson, The Dollywood Foundation

Dear Friends,

The Very Hungry Caterpillar is turning 50 and I will be 90!

It is one of the joys of my life that my book, first published in 1969, continues to delight readers of all ages around the world. China, Croatia, Israel, Egypt, Greece, Japan, Germany, Spain, Russia, Mongolia—all over the planet, children and teachers and parents and grandparents and librarians are reading my story and turning the pages, putting a tiny finger through the hole in a strawberry or a pear, and enjoying the bright, colorful wings of the butterfly when it appears.

I am very, very grateful to every single reader and friend of the caterpillar for these wonderful years together. A golden anniversary for the caterpillar and the butterfly.

Thank you to all, and here's to 50 more!

THE VERY HUNGRY CATERPILLAR

by Eric Carle

PHILOMEL BOOKS

ALSO BY ERIC CARLE

The Very Busy Spider
The Very Quiet Cricket
The Very Lonely Firefly
The Very Clumsy Click Beetle
1, 2, 3 to the Zoo
Animals Animals
Dragons Dragons
Draw Me a Star
Dream Snow
Friends
Little Cloud
Mister Seahorse
The Nonsense Show
"Slowly, Slowly, Slowly," Said the Sloth
Today Is Monday

Copyright © 1969 and 1987 by Eric Carle.
Published by Philomel Books, a division of Penguin Young Readers Group,
345 Hudson Street, New York, NY 10014.
First Published in 1969 by The World Publishing Company,
Cleveland and New York. All rights reserved.
No part of this book may be reproduced in any form without written permission
from the publisher, except for brief passages included in a review. Manufactured in China.
Eric Carle's name and logotype are registered trademarks of Eric Carle.

Library of Congress Cataloging-in-Publication Data
Carle, Eric. The very hungry caterpillar.
Summary: Follows the progress of a very hungry caterpillar as he eats his way through
varied and very large quantity of food, until, full at last, he forms a cocoon around
himself and goes to sleep. [1. Caterpillars-Fiction.] I. Title. PZ7.C2147Ve [E] 79-13202
ISBN 978-0-399-25673-8
Special Markets: 978-1-984-81283-4 Not for resale
2 3 4 5 6 7 8 9 10

This Imagination Library edition is published by Penguin Young Readers, a division
of Penguin Random House, exclusively for Dolly Parton's Imagination Library,
a not-for-profit program designed to inspire a love of reading and learning, sponsored
in part by The Dollywood Foundation. Penguin's trade editions of this work are
available wherever books are sold.

For my sister Christa

In the light of the moon
a little egg lay on a leaf.

One Sunday morning the warm sun came up and—pop!—out of the egg came a tiny and very hungry caterpillar.

He started to look for some food.

On Friday
he ate through
five oranges,
but he was still
hungry.

On Saturday
he ate through
one piece of
chocolate cake, one ice-cream cone, one pickle, one slice of Swiss cheese, one slice of salami,

On Thursday
he ate through
four strawberries,
but he was still
hungry.

one lollipop, one piece of cherry pie, one sausage, one cupcake, and one slice of watermelon.

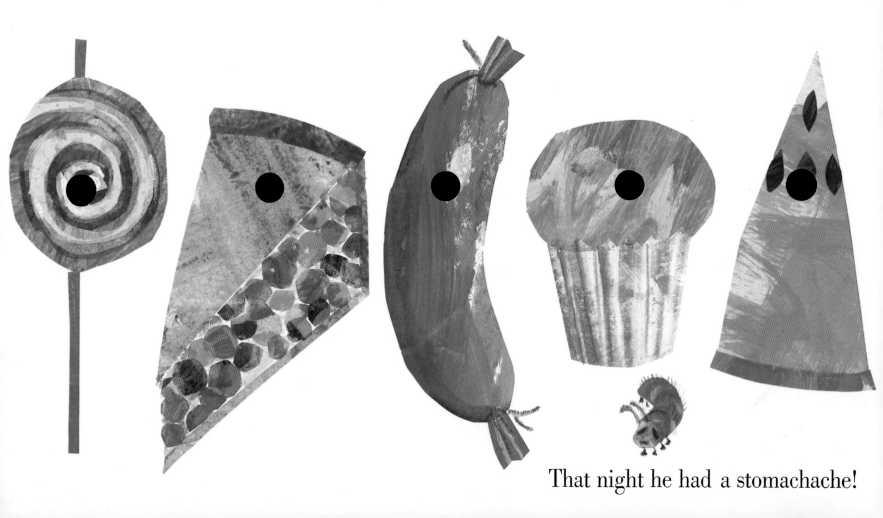

That night he had a stomachache!

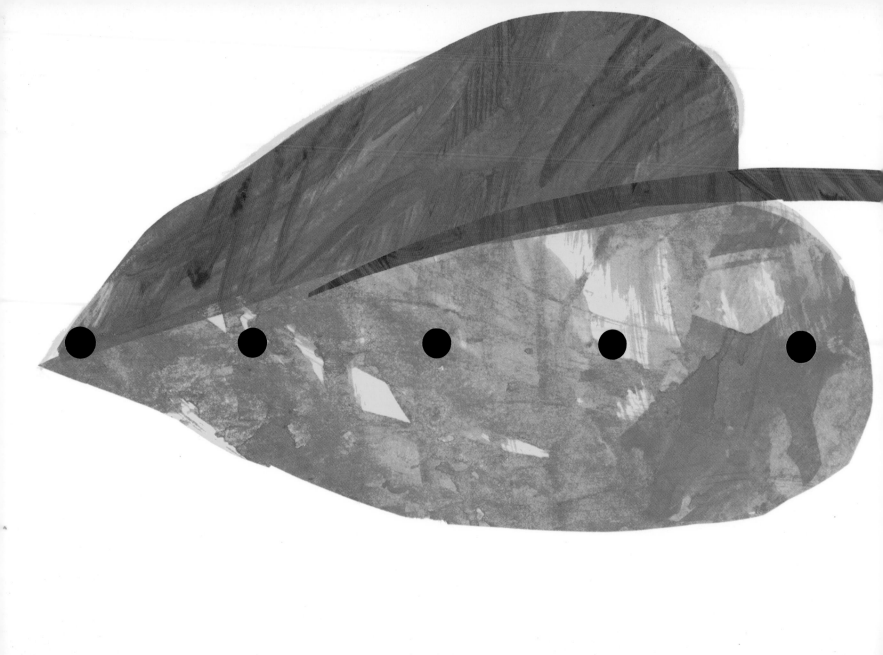

The next day was Sunday again.
The caterpillar ate through
one nice green leaf,
and after that he felt
much better.

Now he wasn't hungry any more—and he wasn't a little caterpillar any more.
He was a big, fat caterpillar.

He built a small house, called a cocoon, around himself. He stayed inside for more than two weeks. Then he nibbled a hole in the cocoon, pushed his way out and . . .

he was a beautiful butterfly!